Pirates of the Kiddy Pool

by Sarah Willson

Illustrated by Bob Roper

SCHOLASTIC INC.

New York   Toronto   London   Auckland   Sydney
Mexico City   New Delhi   Hong Kong   Buenos Aires

Published by Scholastic Inc.,
90 Old Sherman Turnpike, Danbury, CT 06816.

SCHOLASTIC and associated logos are trademarks
and/or registered trademarks of Scholastic Inc.

ISBN 0-439-56291-0

First Scholastic Printing, March 2004

Chapters

Chapter 1
Ship Ahoy! ....Page 9

Chapter 2
Pirates! ....Page 13

Chapter 3
Maroomed! ....Page 24

Chapter 4
Bucket-nears ....Page 29

Chapter 5
Outscoundreled ....Page 34

Chapter 6
The Plan ....Page 44

Chapter 7
Binky Bill's Binky ....Page 50

"Stu, how many times *did* you play to win all these necklaces?" Didi Pickles asked her husband. The Pickles, Finster, and DeVille families were at an amusement park.

"Uh, only sixteen or seventeen games or so," admitted Stu.

"Daddy!" demanded Angelica, "before we go to the water park, I want to ride the Twist & Hurl one more time!"

Drew smiled weakly. "Sure, Princess."

Angelica dragged her father away. The rest of the group headed into the toddler area of the water park.

"We'll be watching you from here!" said
Didi, as she and the other parents sat down
near the edge of the kiddy pool.

"Look, you guys!" said Kimi, pointing.
Chuckie gasped. A huge pirate ship
loomed in front of them.

"I don't like the looks of this," said Chuckie. "Maybe we should go put on more sunblock."

"Aw, come on, Chuckie," said Tommy. "It looks really fun!"

"Smile, kids!" called Stu. He snapped a picture. The kids crowded around to watch it develop. Without warning, Dil snatched the photo and stuck it into his swim diaper.

Stu chuckled. "Oh well, I have plenty
more film. Have fun!" said Stu, as he and Dil
headed back to join the parents watching
from nearby lounge chairs.

"Tommy, what if there's real pirates here?" said Chuckie.

"There aren't, Chuckie. It's just for play . . . "

"Hand over those neckelses," said a gravelly voice behind them.

Chuckie whirled around and found himself facing a large shirt. His gaze moved upward. "I knewed it!" he moaned. "There *are* real pirates here!"

"That's right," said the boy. "This area belongs to me and my mates. We have season passes, so we come here every day. We rule this ship."

"But you can't take our neckelses!" said Kimi. "That's stealing!"

The kid just smirked and
pointed up at the ship.

Mean-looking kids were
aiming water soakers
straight at them.

"We'll letcha go quietly this time," said Binky Bill. "Just hand us those neckelses, and go play somewhere else."

"We better do what he says, you guys," said Tommy to his friends.

The babies surrendered their necklaces. Then they sloshed away from the ship, with Chuckie leading the way.

"And don't come back . . . or else!" said the big kid.

The babies waded to a little island in the middle of a pool. Several kids were already there.

"Hi, there," a toddler said glumly. "You look like you've met Binky Bill."

"Binky Bill?" Tommy echoed.

"Yeah," the kid replied. "He steals binkies from babies just to be mean. And those are his friends, Diaper Dan, Peg-leg Peg, and Long-John Silverspoon."

"They stole my ice cream cone," snuffled another kid.

"They took away the prize my mommy won for me!" said a third.

"Binky Bill and his friends are big pirate bullies," said the first kid. The others nodded. "He hides the stuff he steals in his secret treasure chest."

"We heard he has a huge shark guarding it," whispered the second kid.

"And he won't let anyone play on the
pirate ship," added the third.

"Well, that's just not right!" declared Tommy. Phil, Lil, and Kimi nodded in agreement.

"Let's go make him give us back our toys!" said Kimi.

"I was afraid of that," groaned Chuckie.

"Oh, look at the kids," said Didi to the other parents. "They're having so much fun!"

The babies waded ashore from the island,
then circled back to the ship.

"It looks like nobody's here," whispered Lil.

Suddenly they heard . . .

"Ready . . . aim . . . SQUIRT!!!"

Tommy and his friends were instantly
squirted from all directions. "Follow me!"
yelled Tommy.

"They can't get us here," said Tommy. "Those squirters don't reach . . ."

Suddenly they heard a noise from above. They looked up as a huge bucket tipped, dumping water on their heads.

"MWAH-HA! HA! HA! HA!" cackled Binky Bill.

"What's going on here?" the babies heard someone say. They rubbed the water out of their eyes. It was Angelica.

"Hi, Angelica," said Chuckie in a small voice. "Um, where'd you get that crockydile?"

"My dad tried to knock over some bottles for it, but he couldn't," said Angelica. "So he made the man sell it to us for a lot of monies."

"Cool," said a gravelly voice. "Now, hand it over."

Angelica whirled around to face Binky Bill.

"Careful, Angelica!" cried Lil. "He's not nice! He took our neckelses!"

Angelica's eyes narrowed. "Who do you think you are?"

"His name's Binky Bill," Chuckie supplied helpfully.

Binky Bill pulled the binky out of his mouth and shoved it into his pocket. He just smirked at Angelica.

"*I* was planning on taking those neckelses," said Angelica. "Nobody bosses these babies around but me!"

"Oh, yeah?"

"YEAH!"

"Step over here and say that!" said Binky Bill.

Angelica set down her crocodile and took a few steps toward Binky Bill.

The big bucket tipped again.

WHOOSH!

Before Angelica had time to react, Binky
Bill's friends picked up her crocodile, and
they all dashed away.

"That kid is a pirate, Angelica. He tooked our stuff, too," Chuckie said kindly.

"Some kids told us he's hidden all his stolen treasure around here," added Kimi.

Angelica's eyes flashed.

"Well, then," said Angelica. "We're just gonna go steal the treasure right back. Two can play this pirate game! I'll show him who's the boss of this pirate ship! Come on, babies. Follow me!"

Chapter 6
The Plan

A little while later, Angelica and the babies marched up to Binky Bill. "Give me back my Crocky!" demanded Angelica.

"Mwah-ha-ha-ha-ha!" laughed Binky Bill.
"I hid it. You'll never find it!"
Then suddenly his sneer
changed to an angelic
smile. A woman was
approaching them.

"I think that's his
mom," Tommy whispered
to Angelica.

"There you are, Sweetums!" gushed the woman. "What cute little friends you've made!"

"We're doing a great job sharing our toys, Mumsy!" Binky said sweetly.

"Of course you are, Pumpkin! And Mumsy is so proud of you for going without the binky all day today!" She pinched his cheek lovingly. "You've earned an ice-cream sundae! We'll go just as soon as I finish my magazine, okay, Snookums?"

47

"Hmmm," said Angelica thoughtfully.

"Hey, I got an idea," Tommy said at the same time. But Angelica was already hurrying away. Tommy started to call to her, then turned and headed over to where Dil was dozing.

"Where's Tommy?" Angelica demanded a little while later. The others shrugged. "Okay, then you guys will have to help!" she said.

Chuckie gulped.

"Get their 'tension while I sneak on board!" whispered Angelica. Then she darted up the gangplank.

"So! We beat again!" said Angelica, springing in front of a surprised Binky Bill. "Tell me where the treasure is hidden . . . or else!"

"Or else . . . what?" Binky replied.

"Or else . . . " said Angelica, ". . . I'll have to have a little talk with your mom . . . about binkies!!!"

"You wouldn't dare!" Binky gasped.

"Oh, wouldn't I?" sneered Angelica.

Binky Bill recovered quickly. "She won't believe you!" he said triumphantly. "I'll tell her you're a dirty cotton liar!"

"Well then . . ." Tommy jumped out, startling both of them. "Maybe this will conrinse her!" He held out the photo Stu had taken earlier.

Angelica grinned. "Not bad for a baby,"
she said.

"You win!" croaked Binky Bill. He pulled out a crumpled map. "Here's where I hid the treasure."

"We can't read yet," said Angelica impatiently.

"Me either," admitted Binky. "But all you gots to do is wait 'til the bucket tips, then run past it. Look behind the shark sign."

"Let's roll," said Angelica to Tommy.

"Wait!" called Binky. "What about that binky picture?"

"Promise to be nice to little kids from now on?" asked Tommy.

Binky nodded earnestly.

Tommy handed him the photo.

"Crocky!" shouted Angelica a few minutes later.

"Our neckelses!" said Kimi happily.

"Come on, you guys. We gots to bring all this stuff back to the kids it belongs to," said Tommy.

"Well, for once you babies did something right," said Angelica grudgingly. "Maybe I'll let you keep those neckelses."

"You know something, Tommy?"
said Chuckie a little while later.

"What, Chuckie?" Tommy replied.

"I gots to admit. This place really is . . . "

The big bucket tipped.

". . . kinda fun!" finished Chuckie.